Angel & Elf

Snowy Magic

To

Lowrie

With love from

Jim, Bertha, Peter,

Jennifer & Elizabeth

(Christmas 2007)

For my parents,
who made
Christmas magical!
– S.W.

Published in Great Britain in 2002 by Gullane Children's Books
This paperback edition published in 2002 by

GULLANE
CHILDREN'S BOOKS

Winchester House, 259-269 Old Marylebone Road, London, NW1 5XJ
First published in the USA in 2002 by HarperCollins Children's Books,
a division of HarperCollins Publishers, Inc.

1 3 5 7 9 10 8 6 4 2

Copyright © 2002 by Sam Williams
Published by arrangement with HarperCollins Children's Books,
a division of HarperCollins Publishers, Inc.

The right of Sam Williams to be identified as the author and illustrator
of this work has been asserted by him in accordance with the Copyright,
Designs and Patents Act, 1988.

A CIP record for this title is available from the British Library.

ISBN 1 86233 457 9 hb
ISBN 1 86233 433 1 pb

Printed and bound China

Angel & Elf
Snowy Magic

Sam Williams

GULLANE™
CHILDREN'S BOOKS

Elf opened his front door to collect the milk.

The sky was grey. The air was cold, but it still hadn't snowed.

Then, Elf saw Squirrel and Badger on their way to work.

"Hello," called Elf. "Do you think it might snow today?"
Squirrel and Badger sniffed the air.

"Not today, Elf," they called back.

"Shouldn't you be at work?" shouted Badger.

"I heard the bell a few moments ago."

"Oh, mistletoe!" said Elf. He was late for work.
Elf grabbed one of Angel's Christmas cookies
and ran all the way to Santa's workshop.

Elf had a busy day at the toy workshop.
He had been painting little wooden engines.

On his way home, Elf began to feel a little sad.
"Still no sign of snow," he sighed.
Then, he saw his best friend, Angel.

"Hello, Elf," said Angel. "You don't look very happy."

"Hello, Angel," said Elf. "I *wish* it would snow.

It just isn't the same without snow."

"I could magic some snow," said Angel.

"Yes, yes!" shouted Elf.

His little pointy ears started to waggle.

"Can you really do that?" Elf asked excitedly.

"I can try," said Angel.

Angel waved her wand and flapped her little wings
and rose off the ground.

In a short time, Elf felt two white, fluffy snowflakes
kiss his cold cheeks.

Great big snowflakes followed.

"Yippeeeee!" said Elf. "It worked!"

Angel was very pleased with herself.

She had never done that before.

Bigger snowflakes fell heavier than before.
The snow lay thick and deep all around them.
Angel and Elf jumped and skipped
and fell about in the snow.

Before long, families of snow people appeared.
They laughed and threw snowballs at each other.

Angel and Elf joined them.

The snow fell faster and became deeper and deeper.

Nobody heard the small voices calling out for help.

"Help!" came the voices again, louder than before.

Angel, Elf and the snow people stopped playing and listened.

It was the squirrels.

"Help!" they cried. "Our home is gone!"

They pointed to their tree that was now buried
in the deep snow that Angel had made.

"What shall we do, Elf?" cried Angel.

"Magic the snow away," said Elf.

But Angel's wand was also hidden
beneath the deep snow.

Now everyone was worried.

Even Santa's workshop had almost disappeared.

The snow kept falling faster and faster.

"I wish Santa was here," said Elf.

First, they heard the faint jingle of bells.

Then, from out of the snowy sky,

came Santa riding on a reindeer.

With one gentle touch of his nose,
Santa made all the snow disappear.
The snow people vanished, too.
Now the squirrels' home was safe.

"Sorry, Santa." said Angel and Elf.

"It was all my fault," said Angel.

"No, no," interrupted Elf. "It was my fault.
I couldn't wait for it to snow."
"No harm is done, Elf," laughed Santa.
"There is a great deal to do, so I must be going
and you two should go and get some sleep."

Elf helped Angel find her wand.

Then, they said they were sorry to the squirrels.

Soon it was time for bed.

"Good night, Elf," said Angel, as she flew away.

"Good night, Angel," called Elf.

Early the next morning, there
was a loud knock on Elf's door.
"It's snowing!" called Angel.

Elf couldn't believe
his tired little eyes.

"Did you do this?" asked Elf.

"No, I didn't, you silly elf," laughed Angel.

"It did it all by itself. It's going to be a
white Christmas after all, Elf!"

Merry
Christmas,
everyone!

Other Gullane Children's Books for you to enjoy

Auntie Claus

Elise Primavera

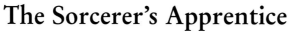

Harry and the Snow King

Ian Whybrow • Adrian Reynolds

The Sorcerer's Apprentice

Sally Grindley • Thomas Taylor

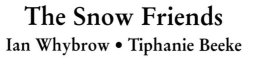

The Snow Friends

Ian Whybrow • Tiphanie Beeke